THIS CANDLEWICK BOOK BELONGS TO:

_____

_____

_____

_____

For Bess

Copyright © 1998 by Kim Lewis

First U.S. paperback edition 2000

The Library of Congress has cataloged the
hardcover edition as follows:

Lewis, Kim.
Just like Floss / Kim Lewis.—1st U.S. ed.
p.   cm.

Summary: Floss the sheep dog has a litter of puppies and Floss's
owners want to keep the one that is just like Floss.
ISBN 0-7636-0684-7 (hardcover)
[1. Border collies—Fiction.   2. Dogs—Fiction.   3. Animals—Infancy.]   I. Title.
PZ7.L58723Ju   1998
[E]—dc21   98-4954
ISBN 0-7636-1079-8 (paperback)

10 9 8 7 6 5 4 3 2 1

Printed in Hong Kong / China

This book was typeset in Sabon.
The pictures were done in colored pencil.

Candlewick Press
2067 Massachusetts Avenue
Cambridge, Massachusetts 02140

Just like Floss

KIM LEWIS

CANDLEWICK PRESS
CAMBRIDGE, MASSACHUSETTS

One night in winter
Floss lay in the hay
with her newborn
collie puppies.
She licked them dry
and kept them warm
as snow fell
against the barn.

"Dad, can we
    keep a puppy?"
the children asked.
"Maybe," their father
said. "We could use
another collie just like
Floss to work with
the sheep on the farm."

The children watched
the puppies grow and gave
each one a name.

"Dad, we love them all," they said.
"Which one would be the best?"
"Wait and see,"
their father said.

Bess and Nell played tug of war.

Cap and Jack played hide-and-seek.

The littlest, Sam, kept following Floss.

She licked his ears and nose and barked.

"What does Floss tell Sam?"

the children asked.

Floss went back
to work with Dad,
gathering sheep
on the farm.
"Come on, pups!"
the children said
and took them all
outside. Bess and Nell
played tug of war.
Cap and Jack played
hide-and-seek.
Sam went looking
for his mother.

Sam ran in the snow.
He jumped in the drifts
by a hole in the fence.
He chased after snowflakes
into the field. The sheep looked
up at the sight of a puppy.
Curious, they came closer.

Sheep gathered around and
stared at Sam. Their breath
blew hot in the cold snowy air.
Sam looked at the big
woolly shapes with their
hard black heads
and horns.

One ewe put her head down
to sniff at Sam. She was big
and Sam was little. Sam wanted
to run, but he stayed very still.
He looked in the old ewe's eyes.

Slowly the ewe
began to back away.
Sam crouched low
and started to run.
With a clicking of heels,
all the sheep scattered.
"Sam!" cried the children.
"Sam, come here!"

Sam tripped in the snow
and tumbled over.
The children caught the snowy puppy.
"Big brave Sam!" they said and carried
him back to the barn with Cap
and Jack, Bess and Nell.

Floss was waiting at the barn
with Dad. She licked Sam's
cold wet ears and nose.
"Sam's not afraid of sheep!"
said the children.
"He'll be just like Floss."
"Then we'll keep Sam,"
said Dad, "and find
good homes for all
the others."

The children hugged
the little puppy.
"And we'll love you, Sam,"
they said,
"just like Floss."

KIM LEWIS lives on a working sheep farm in England. "It is a moment of magic when a young border collie comes to know what its job is," she says. "You can suddenly see something click—good border collies naturally know how to herd sheep."